Lilly & Friends

KEVIN HENKES

Lilly & Friends

A Picture Book Treasury

GREENWILLOW BOOKS
An Imprint of HarperCollins*Publishers*

Library of Congress Control Number: 2020937640

ISBN 978-0-06-299551-3 (hardback)

20 21 22 23 24 SCP 10 9 8 7 6 5 4 3 2 1

Greenwillow Books

"Wow," said Mr. Slinger.
That was just about all he could say. "Wow."

Contents

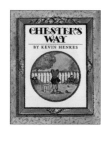

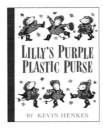
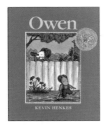

MEET
Lilly & Friends

Lilly and her friends are mice. They have long tails and round ears, and they love cheese. They have brothers and sisters and cousins and friends and mothers and fathers and grandparents and teachers and neighbors.

In the nine stories in this book, Lilly and her friends go on adventures, learn new things, and laugh a lot. They are happy, sad, scared, angry, fearless, imaginative, regretful, brave, kind, surprised, mischievous, worried, helpful, funny, stubborn, sly, generous, silly, and smart. They love school and parties and parades and drawing and riding bikes and sleepovers and secret disguises and tasty snacks.

Do they have fun? Yes!

Do they make mistakes? Yes!

Do they get into trouble? Yes!

Will they make you laugh? Yes!

Will you ever forget them? No!

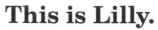

This is Lilly.

And these are her friends.

Welcome to the world
of Lilly and friends . . .
they are so happy you are here!

A WEEKEND WITH WENDELL

BY KEVIN HENKES

GREENWILLOW BOOKS NEW YORK

On Friday afternoon Wendell's parents dropped him
off at Sophie's house.
"Wendell's going to spend the weekend with us," said
    Sophie's mother, "while his parents visit relatives out of town."
"Oh boy!" said Wendell.
    Sophie didn't say anything.

After a snack, Sophie helped Wendell carry his sleeping bag and suitcase upstairs.

"Well, what are we going to do now?" asked Wendell. "Do you have any toys?"

Sophie pointed to her toy chest.

"Is that all you've got?" said Wendell. "I've got a million times more than that. What else is there to do around here?"

"We could play house?" said Sophie.

"Only if I can make the rules," said Wendell.

So they played house and Wendell made the rules.
He was the father, the mother, and the five children.
Sophie was the dog.

Then they played hospital.

Wendell was the doctor, the nurse, and the patient.

Sophie was the desk clerk.

When they pretended they worked in a bakery,
Wendell was the baker and Sophie was a sweet roll.
"Isn't this fun?" said Wendell.
Sophie didn't say anything.

At dinner Wendell said that he was allergic to anything
green—so he didn't have to eat his vegetables.
And then, when Sophie wasn't looking, he scooped the
whipped cream off her dessert.

"When is Wendell leaving?" whispered Sophie.

"Soon," said her mother.

"Soon," said her father.

After Sophie's parents tucked Sophie in her bed, zipped
Wendell in his sleeping bag, kissed them both, and
turned off the light, Wendell grabbed his flashlight and
shone it right in Sophie's eyes.
"SEE YOU TOMORROW!" he said smiling.

Sophie shut her eyes. "I can't wait for Wendell to go home," she said to herself.

On Saturday morning, when Sophie woke up, there was a lumpy blue monster jumping up and down on her bed. It was Wendell.

She felt something pinch her leg at breakfast.
It was Wendell.

She heard scary noises coming from the broom closet.
It was Wendell.

Wendell used Sophie's crayons and left them on the porch so they melted.

At lunch Wendell finger-painted with his
peanut butter and jelly.
"Isn't this fun?" said Wendell.
Sophie didn't say anything.

"When is Wendell leaving?" whispered Sophie.

"Soon," said her mother.

"Soon," said her father.

At bedtime, when Sophie put her head on her pillow, she heard something crunch. It was a note from Wendell. It said, "SEE YOU TOMORROW!" Sophie shut her eyes. "I can't wait for Wendell to go home," she said to herself.

Before Wendell's parents picked him up on Sunday
morning, he tried to make a long-distance call,

he wrote his name on the bathroom mirror
with toothpaste,

and he gave Sophie a new hairdo with shaving cream.

"Want to go outside to help me wash this off?" asked
 Sophie. "We could play fire fighter."
"Oh boy!" said Wendell.

So they played fire fighter—and *Sophie* made the rules.
She was the fire chief. Wendell was the burning building.
"Isn't this fun?" said Sophie.
Wendell didn't say anything.

"Do I get to be the fire chief?" asked Wendell.
"Maybe," said Sophie.

Soon Wendell and Sophie didn't care who was
the fire chief or who was the burning building.

"Time to go!" said Sophie's mother.

"Time to go!" said Sophie's father.

"Already?" said Wendell.

"Already?" said Sophie.

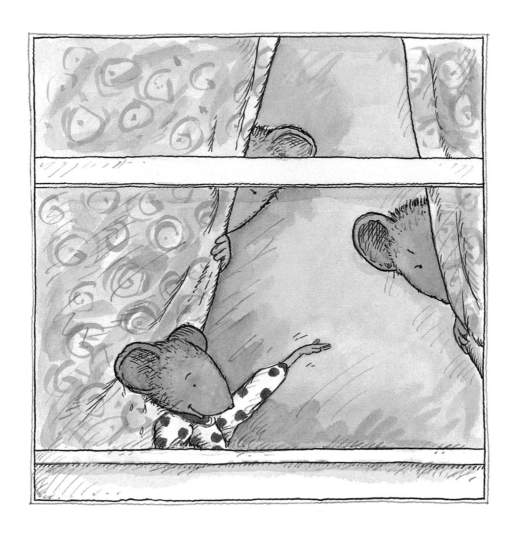

"When is Wendell coming back?" asked Sophie.

"Never!" said her mother.

"Never!" said her father.

That afternoon, when Wendell unpacked his suitcase, he heard something crunch. It was a note from Sophie. It said, "I HOPE I SEE YOU SOON!"

SHEILA RAE, THE BRAVE

by Kevin Henkes

Greenwillow Books • New York

Sheila Rae wasn't afraid of anything.

She wasn't afraid of the dark.

She wasn't afraid of thunder and lightning.

And she wasn't afraid of the big black dog
at the end of the block.

At dinner, Sheila Rae made believe that the cherries
in her fruit cocktail were the eyes of dead bears,
and she ate five of them.

At school, Sheila Rae giggled when the principal walked by.

And when her classmate Wendell stole her jump rope
during recess, Sheila Rae tied him up until the bell rang.
"I am very brave," Sheila Rae said, patting herself on
the back.

Sheila Rae stepped on every crack in the sidewalk without fear.

When her sister, Louise, said there was a monster in the closet, Sheila Rae attacked it.

And she rode her bicycle no-handed with her eyes closed.
"Yea! Yea! Sheila Rae!" her friends yelled,
clapping their hands.

One day, Sheila Rae decided to walk home
from school a new way. Louise was afraid to.
"You're too brave for me," Louise said.

"You're always such a scaredy-cat," Sheila Rae called.
"Am not," whispered Louise.

Sheila Rae started off, skipping.
"I am brave," she sang. "I am fearless."

She stepped on every crack.

She walked backwards with her eyes closed.

She growled at stray dogs,

and bared her teeth at stray cats.

And she pretended that the trees were evil creatures.
She climbed up them and broke their fingers off.
Snap, snap, snap.

Sheila Rae walked and walked.

She turned corners.

She crossed streets.

It suddenly occurred to Sheila Rae
that nothing looked familiar.

Sheila Rae heard frightening noises.
They sounded worse than thunder.

She thought horrible thoughts.
   They were worse than anything she had ever imagined.
"I am brave," Sheila Rae tried to convince herself.
"I am fearless."

The sounds became more frightening.
The thoughts became more horrible.
Sheila Rae sat down on a rock and cried.
"Help," she sniffed.

She thought of her mother and her father and Louise.
"Mother! Father! Louise!" she cried.

"Here I am," a voice said.

"Louise!" Sheila Rae hugged her sister.
"We're lost," Sheila Rae said.
"No, we're not," said Louise. "I know the
way home. Follow me!"

Louise stepped on every crack.

She walked backwards with her eyes closed.

She growled at stray dogs, and bared
her teeth at stray cats.

And she pretended that the trees were evil creatures.
She jumped up and broke their fingers off.
Snap, snap, snap.
Sheila Rae walked quietly behind her.

They walked and walked.

They crossed streets.

They turned corners.

Soon their house could be seen between the trees.
Sheila Rae grabbed Louise and dashed up the street.

When they reached their own yard and the gate
was closed behind them, Sheila Rae said,
"Louise, you are brave. You are fearless."

"We both are," said Louise.
And they walked backwards into the house
with their eyes closed.

CHESTER'S WAY

by Kevin Henkes

Greenwillow Books • *New York*

Hello, my name is Chester.
I like croquet and peanut butter
and making my bed.

CHESTER had his own way of doing things....

He always cut his sandwiches
diagonally.

He always got out of bed
on the same side.

And he never left the house
without double-knotting his shoes.

Chester always had the same thing for breakfast—toast with jam and peanut butter.

And he always carried a miniature first-aid kit in his back pocket. Just in case.

"You definitely have a mind of your own," said Chester's mother. "That's one way to put it," said Chester's father.

Chester's best friend Wilson was exactly the same way. That's why they were best friends.

Chester wouldn't play baseball unless Wilson played, and they never swung at the first pitch or slid headfirst.

Wilson wouldn't ride his bike unless Chester wanted to, and they always used hand signals.

If Chester was hungry, Wilson was too, but they rarely ate between meals.

"Some days I can't tell those two apart," said Wilson's mother. "Me either," said Wilson's father.

ADVANCED CROQUET TIPS

Chester and Wilson, Wilson and Chester. That's the way it was.

They loved to go on picnics. Once, when Wilson accidently swallowed a watermelon seed and cried because he was afraid that a watermelon plant would grow inside him, Chester swallowed one, too.

"Don't worry," said Chester. "Now, if you grow a watermelon plant, I'll grow one, too."

Chester duplicated his Christmas list every year and gave a copy to Wilson, because they always wanted the same things anyway.

For Halloween, they always dressed as things that went together—salt and pepper shakers, two mittens on a string, ham and eggs.

"They really are two peas in a pod," said Chester's mother.

"Looks like it," said Chester's father.

In spring, Chester and Wilson shared the same umbrella.

In winter, they never threw snowballs at each other.

In fall, they raked leaves together.

And in summer, they reminded each other
to wear sunscreen, so they wouldn't burn.

★ 77 ★

Chester and Wilson, Wilson and Chester.
That's the way it was.

And then Lilly moved into the neighborhood.

I'm Lilly!
I am the Queen!
I like EVERYTHING!

LILLY had <u>her</u> own way of doing things....

She wore band-aids all over her
arms and legs, to look brave.

She talked backwards to herself
sometimes, so no one would
know what she was saying.

And she never left the house
without one of her
nifty disguises.

Lilly waved at all the cars that passed by, even if she didn't know who was in them.

And she always carried a loaded squirt gun in her back pocket. Just in case.

"She definitely has a mind of her own," said Chester.
"That's one way to put it," said Wilson.

When Lilly asked Chester and Wilson to play, they
said they were busy.

When she called them up on the phone, they disguised
their voices and said they weren't home.

If Lilly was walking on one side of the street, Chester and Wilson crossed to the other and hid.

"She's something else," said Chester.
"Looks like it," said Wilson.

One day, while Chester and Wilson were practicing their hand signals, some older boys rode by, popping wheelies. They circled Chester and Wilson and yelled personal remarks.

Chester and Wilson didn't know what to do. Just when they were about to give up hope, a fierce-looking cat with horrible fangs jumped out of the bushes and frightened the older boys away.

"Are you who I think you are?" Chester asked the cat.
"Of course," the cat replied.

"Thank you, Lilly," said Chester.

"You're welcome, Chester," said Lilly.

"Thank you, Lilly," said Wilson.

"You're welcome, Wilson," said Lilly.

"I'm glad you were wearing a disguise," said Chester.

"And I'm glad you had your squirt gun," said Wilson.

"I always do," said Lilly. "Just in case."

Afterward, Chester invited
Lilly over for lunch.
"You have a Muscle Mouse
 cup?!" said Lilly.
"Of course," said Chester.
"I do, too!" said Lilly.
"Same here," said Wilson.

Chester and Wilson cut their
sandwiches diagonally. Lilly asked
Chester's mother if she had cookie
cutters, and she made stars and
flowers and bells.
"That's neat!" said Chester.
"Wow!" said Wilson.

That night, Lilly invited Chester
and Wilson to sleep over.
"You have a night light?!" said
Chester.
"Of course," said Lilly.
"I do, too!" said Chester.
"Same here," said Wilson.

Chester and Wilson wanted toast
with jam and peanut butter for
breakfast the next morning.
"Boring," said Lilly. "Try this
instead."
"This is good!" said Chester.
"Wow!" said Wilson.

After that, when Lilly asked
Chester and Wilson to play,
they said yes.

When she called them up on
the phone, they had pleasant
conversations.

And if Lilly was walking on one
side of the street, Chester and
Wilson waved and ran to catch
up with her.

Chester and Wilson taught Lilly hand signals. And she taught them how to pop wheelies.

Lilly taught Chester and Wilson how to talk backwards. And they taught her how to double-knot her shoes.

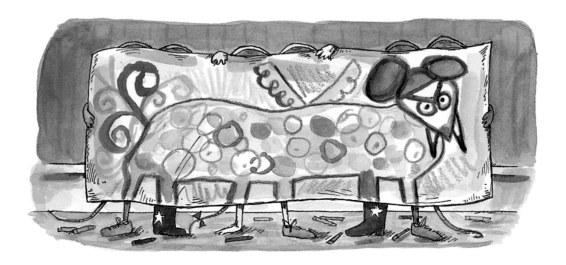

"Some days I can't tell those three apart," said
Lilly's mother.
"Me either," said Lilly's father.

Chester and Wilson and Lilly, Lilly and Wilson
and Chester. That's the way it was.

For Halloween, they dressed as The Three Blind Mice.

For Christmas, Lilly gave Chester and Wilson nifty disguises. And they gave her a box of multi-colored shoelaces—extra long for double-knotting.

They loved to go on picnics. When Chester and Wilson told Lilly about how they had each swallowed a watermelon seed once, Lilly swallowed <u>three</u> of them. "I'll grow a watermelon plant for each of us," she said.

In spring, Chester and Wilson and Lilly shared the same umbrella.

In winter, they never threw snowballs at each other.

In fall, they raked leaves together.

And in summer, they reminded each other to wear sunscreen, so they wouldn't burn.

Chester and Wilson and Lilly,
Lilly and Wilson and Chester.
That's the way it was....

And then Victor moved into the neighborhood...

· J U L I U S ·
THE BABY OF THE WORLD

BY KEVIN HENKES

GREENWILLOW BOOKS • NEW YORK

HOORAY!

WE'RE HAVING A BABY!

THESE ARE FOR THE BABY!

Before Julius was born, Lilly was the best
big sister in the world.
She gave him things.
She told him secrets.
And she sang lullabies to him every night.

After Julius was born, it was a different story.
Lilly took her things back.
She pinched his tail.
And she yelled insulting comments into his crib.

"I am the queen," said Lilly. "And I hate Julius."

But her parents loved him.
They kissed his wet pink nose.
They admired his small black eyes.
And they stroked his sweet white fur.

Lilly thought his wet pink nose was slimy.
She thought his small black eyes were beady.
And she thought his sweet white fur was not so sweet.
Especially when he needed his diaper changed.
"Julius is the baby of the world," chimed Lilly's parents.
"Disgusting," said Lilly.

Lilly had to share her room with Julius.
"After Julius goes away, do I get my room
  back?" she asked.
"Julius isn't going anywhere," said Lilly's mother.
And he didn't.
He stayed and stayed and stayed.

Lilly was supposed to be very quiet while Julius slept.
"After Julius goes away, can I talk like a normal person
again?" she shouted.
"Julius isn't going anywhere," said Lilly's father.
And he didn't.
He stayed and stayed and stayed.

"We want Julius to grow up to be as extraordinary as you,"
said Lilly's mother, "so we must tell him constantly how
beautiful he is and how much we love him."

When no one was looking, Lilly had her own idea.

"We want Julius to grow up to be as clever as you," said
Lilly's father, "so we must sing him his numbers and letters
whenever possible."

When no one was looking, Lilly had her own idea.

Lilly's parents were more than a bit doubtful about
leaving the two of them alone together.
Lilly tried to frighten Julius with her nifty disguises.
She learned magic and tried to make him disappear.
When that didn't work, she simply pretended that he
didn't exist.

Lilly spent more time than usual in the uncooperative chair.

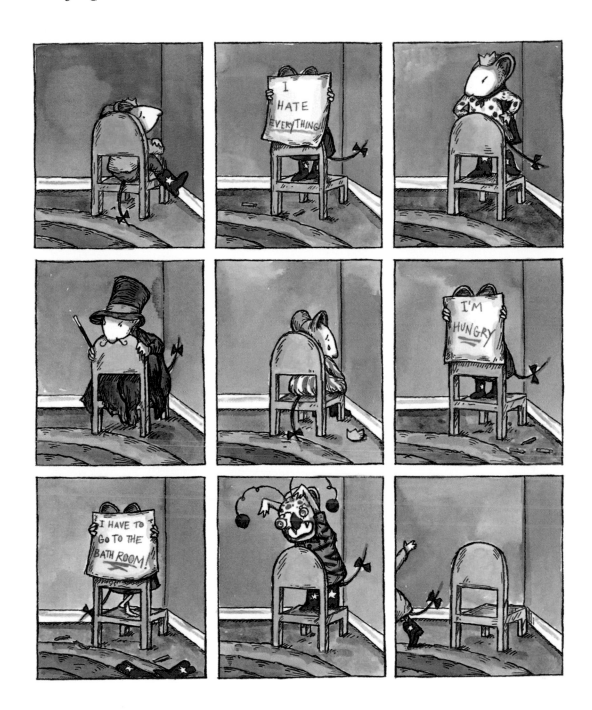

Lilly's parents showered her with hugs and kisses
and treats of all shapes and sizes.
They even let her stay up fifteen minutes later every night.
It didn't matter. Nothing worked.

"I am the queen," said Lilly. "And I hate Julius."

But her parents loved him.
They kissed his wet pink nose.
They admired his small black eyes.
And they stroked his sweet white fur.

"Julius is the baby of the world," chimed Lilly's parents.
"Disgusting," said Lilly.

Lilly's parents were amused when Julius blew a bubble.
"Can you believe it?!" they exclaimed.
   But if Lilly did the exact same thing, they said,
"Lilly, let's mind our manners, please."

Lilly's parents were dazzled when Julius babbled and gurgled.
"Such a vocabulary!" they exclaimed.
   But if Lilly did the exact same thing, they said,
"Lilly, let's act our age, please."

Lilly's parents were amazed when Julius screamed.
"What lung capacity!" they exclaimed.
But if Lilly did the exact same thing, they said,
"Lilly, let's restrain ourselves, please."

One morning, while Lilly was busy playing opera,
her mother said, "Why don't you put some of that verbal
exuberance to good use? Why don't you tell Julius
a nice story?"
"He's too little to understand a story," said Lilly.
"He can understand it in his own way," said Lilly's mother.
"Okay," said Lilly, smiling.

"JULIUS, THE GERM OF THE WORLD.
  BY ME," said Lilly.
"Once upon a time," said Lilly, "there was a baby.
  His name was Julius.
  Julius was really a germ.
  Julius was like dust under your bed.
  If he was a number, he would be zero.
  If he was a food, he would be a raisin.
  Zero is nothing.
  A raisin tastes like dirt.
  The End," said Lilly.

The story earned her ten minutes in the uncooperative chair.

Lilly warned her friends Chester and Wilson and Victor about babies. "Trust me, they're dreadful," she said.

She warned strangers about babies, too.
"You will live to regret that bump under your dress," she said.

Lilly ran away seven times in one morning.
"I'm *really* leaving this time," she called.
"Who knows where they'll find me."

The same afternoon Lilly had a tea party and everyone came.
Everyone but Julius.
"His invitation must have been lost in the mail," she explained.

Lilly had glorious dreams about Julius.

And ghastly nightmares, too.

Lilly's parents showered her with compliments and praise and niceties of all shapes and sizes.
They even let her drink her juice out of the antique china cup.
It didn't matter. Nothing worked.

"I am the queen," said Lilly. "And I hate Julius."

But her parents loved him.
They kissed his wet pink nose.
They admired his small black eyes.
And they stroked his sweet white fur.

"Julius is the baby of the world," chimed Lilly's parents.
"Disgusting," said Lilly.

When Lilly's mother felt up to it, she planned
a festive celebration in honor of Julius.
All the relatives came. There was quite a spread.
"What's the big deal?" said Lilly. "Haven't they
all seen a silly lump before?"

Apparently not. All afternoon the relatives hovered
over Julius.
They kissed his wet pink nose.
They admired his small black eyes.
And they stroked his sweet white fur.

"Disgusting," said Cousin Garland.

"What?" said Lilly.

"Julius," said Cousin Garland. "I think his wet pink nose
is slimy. I think his small black eyes are beady.
And I think his sweet white fur is not so sweet.
He needs his diaper changed."

Lilly's nose twitched.
Her eyes narrowed.
Her fur stood on end.
And her tail quivered.

"You're talking about my brother," said Lilly.
"And for your information, his nose is shiny,
   his eyes are sparkly, and his fur smells like perfume."

Cousin Garland was speechless.

"He can blow bubbles," continued Lilly. "He can babble
   and gurgle. And he can scream better than anyone."

Cousin Garland tried to slink out of the room.

"Stop!" said Lilly. "I am the queen. Watch me closely."

Lilly picked up Julius.
She kissed his wet pink nose.
She admired his small black eyes.
And she stroked his sweet white fur.

"Your turn," said Lilly, handing Julius over to Cousin Garland.
"Kiss! Admire! Stroke!" Lilly commanded.

"Now repeat after me," said Lilly. "Julius is the
baby of the world."
"Julius is the baby of the world," said Cousin Garland.
"Louder!" said Lilly.
"JULIUS IS THE BABY OF THE WORLD!"

And from then on, he was. In everyone's opinion.
Especially in Lilly's.

Chrysanthemum

by Kevin Henkes

Greenwillow Books

New York

The day she was born was the happiest day
in her parents' lives.
"She's perfect," said her mother.
"Absolutely," said her father.
And she was.
She was absolutely perfect.

"Her name must be everything she is," said her mother.

"Her name must be absolutely perfect," said her father.

And it was.

Chrysanthemum. Her parents named her Chrysanthemum.

Chrysanthemum grew and grew and grew.
And when she was old enough to appreciate it,
Chrysanthemum loved her name.

She loved the way it sounded when her mother woke her up.
She loved the way it sounded when her father called her for
dinner.
And she loved the way it sounded when she whispered it to
herself in the bathroom mirror.
Chrysanthemum, Chrysanthemum, Chrysanthemum.

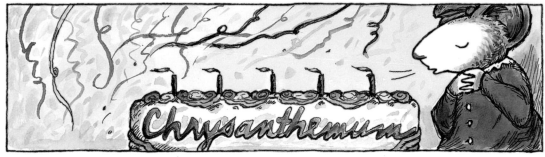

Chrysanthemum loved the way her name looked when it was
written with ink on an envelope.
She loved the way it looked when it was written with icing
on her birthday cake.
And she loved the way it looked when she wrote it herself
with her fat orange crayon.
Chrysanthemum, Chrysanthemum, Chrysanthemum.

Chrysanthemum thought her name was absolutely perfect.
And then she started school.

On the first day, Chrysanthemum wore her sunniest dress
and her brightest smile. She ran all the way.
"Hooray!" said Chrysanthemum. "School!"

But when Mrs. Chud took roll call, everyone giggled upon hearing Chrysanthemum's name.

"It's so *long*," said Jo.

"It scarcely fits on your name tag," said Rita, pointing.

"I'm named after my grandmother," said Victoria.

"You're named after a *flower*!"

Chrysanthemum wilted.

She did not think her name was absolutely perfect.

She thought it was absolutely dreadful.

The rest of the day was not much better.
During naptime Victoria raised her hand and informed
Mrs. Chud that Chrysanthemum's name was spelled with
thirteen letters.
"That's exactly half as many letters as there are in the *entire*
alphabet!" Victoria explained.
"Thank you for sharing that with us, Victoria," said
Mrs. Chud. "Now put your head down."

"If I had a name like yours, I'd change it," Victoria said
as the students lined up to go home.

I wish I could, thought Chrysanthemum miserably.

"Welcome home!" said her mother.

"Welcome home!" said her father.

"School is no place for me," said Chrysanthemum. "My name is too long. It scarcely fits on my name tag. And I'm named after a *flower*!"

"Oh, pish," said her mother. "Your name is beautiful."

"And precious and priceless and fascinating and winsome," said her father.

"It's everything you are," said her mother.

"Absolutely perfect," said her father.

Chrysanthemum felt much better after her favorite dinner
(macaroni and cheese with ketchup) and an evening filled
with hugs and kisses and Parcheesi.

That night Chrysanthemum dreamed that her name was Jane.
It was an extremely pleasant dream.

The next morning Chrysanthemum wore her most comfortable jumper. She walked to school as slowly as she could. She dragged her feet in the dirt.

Chrysanthemum, Chrysanthemum, Chrysanthemum, she wrote.

"She even *looks* like a flower," said Victoria, as
   Chrysanthemum entered the playground.
"Let's pick her," said Rita, pointing.
"Let's smell her," said Jo.

Chrysanthemum wilted.
She did not think her name was absolutely perfect.
She thought it was absolutely dreadful.

The rest of the day was not much better.

During naptime Victoria raised her hand and said,
"A chrysanthemum is a flower. It lives in a garden with worms
and other dirty things."

"Thank you for sharing that with us, Victoria," said Mrs. Chud.
"Now put your head down."

"I just cannot believe your name," Victoria said as the students lined up to go home.

Neither can I, thought Chrysanthemum miserably.

"Welcome home!" said her mother.

"Welcome home!" said her father.

"School is no place for me," said Chrysanthemum. "They said I even *look* like a flower. They pretended to pick me and smell me."

"Oh, pish," said her mother. "They're just jealous."

"And envious and begrudging and discontented and jaundiced," said her father.

"Who wouldn't be jealous of a name like yours?" said her mother.

"After all, it's absolutely perfect," said her father.

Chrysanthemum felt a trifle better after her favorite dessert
(chocolate cake with buttercream frosting) and another evening
filled with hugs and kisses and Parcheesi.

That night Chrysanthemum dreamed that she really *was*
a chrysanthemum.

She sprouted leaves and petals. Victoria picked her and
plucked the leaves and petals one by one until there was
nothing left but a scrawny stem.

It was the worst nightmare of Chrysanthemum's life.

Chrysanthemum wore her outfit with seven pockets the
next morning.
She loaded the pockets with her most prized possessions
and her good-luck charms.
Chrysanthemum took the longest route possible to school.
She stopped and stared at each and every flower.
"Chrysanthemum, Chrysanthemum, Chrysanthemum,"
the flowers seemed to say.

That morning the students were introduced to Mrs. Twinkle,
the music teacher.

Her voice was like something out of a dream, as was everything
else about her.

The students were speechless.

They thought Mrs. Twinkle was an indescribable wonder.

They went out of their way to make a nice impression.

Mrs. Twinkle led the students in scales.

Then she assigned roles for the class musicale.

Victoria was chosen as the dainty Fairy Queen.

Rita was chosen as the spiffy Butterfly Princess.

Jo was chosen as the all-important Pixie-messenger.

And Chrysanthemum was chosen as a daisy.

"Chrysanthemum's a daisy! Chrysanthemum's a daisy!"
Jo, Rita, and Victoria chanted, thinking it was wildly funny.

Chrysanthemum wilted.
She did not think her name was absolutely perfect.
She thought it was absolutely dreadful.

"What's so humorous?" asked Mrs. Twinkle.

"Chrysanthemum!" was the answer.

"Her name is so *long*," said Jo.

"It scarcely fits on her name tag," said Rita, pointing.

"I'm named after my grandmother," said Victoria.

"She's named after a *flower*!"

"*My* name is long," said Mrs. Twinkle.

"It *is*?" said Jo.

"*My* name would scarcely fit on a name tag," said Mrs. Twinkle.

"It *would*?" said Rita, pointing.

"*And*—" said Mrs. Twinkle, "*I'm* named after a flower, too!"

"You *are*?" said Victoria.

"Yes," said Mrs. Twinkle. "My name is Delphinium.
Delphinium Twinkle. And if my baby is a girl, I'm considering
Chrysanthemum as a name. I think it's absolutely perfect."

Chrysanthemum could scarcely believe her ears.
She blushed.
She beamed.
She bloomed.
Chrysanthemum, Chrysanthemum, Chrysanthemum.

Jo, Rita, and Victoria looked at Chrysanthemum longingly.

"Call me Marigold," said Jo.
"I'm Carnation," said Rita, pointing.
"My name is Lily of the Valley," said Victoria.

Chrysanthemum did not *think* her name was absolutely perfect.
She *knew* it!

EPILOGUE:

Overall, the class musicale was a huge success.

Chrysanthemum was absolutely perfect as a daisy.

Victoria made the only mistake: She completely forgot her lines
as the dainty Fairy Queen.

Chrysanthemum thought it was wildly funny, and she giggled
throughout the entire Dance of the Flowers.

Eventually, Mrs. Twinkle gave birth to a healthy baby girl.
And, of course, she named her Chrysanthemum.

Owen

· KEVIN HENKES ·

GREENWILLOW BOOKS
NEW YORK

Owen had a fuzzy yellow blanket.

He'd had it since he was a baby.

He loved it with all his heart.

"Fuzzy goes where I go," said Owen.

And Fuzzy did.

Upstairs, downstairs, in-between.

Inside, outside, upside down.

"Fuzzy likes what I like," said Owen.

And Fuzzy did.

Orange juice, grape juice, chocolate milk.

Ice cream, peanut butter, applesauce cake.

"Isn't he getting a little old to be carrying that thing around?" asked Mrs. Tweezers. "Haven't you heard of the Blanket Fairy?"

Owen's parents hadn't.

Mrs. Tweezers filled them in.

That night Owen's parents told Owen to put Fuzzy under
his pillow.

In the morning Fuzzy would be gone, but the Blanket Fairy
would leave an absolutely wonderful, positively perfect,
especially terrific big-boy gift in its place.

Owen stuffed Fuzzy inside his pajama pants
and went to sleep.

"No Blanket Fairy," said Owen in the morning.

"No kidding," said Owen's mother.

"No wonder," said Owen's father.

"Fuzzy's dirty," said Owen's mother.

"Fuzzy's torn and ratty," said Owen's father.

"No," said Owen. "Fuzzy is perfect."

And Fuzzy was.

Fuzzy played Captain Plunger with Owen.

Fuzzy helped Owen become invisible.

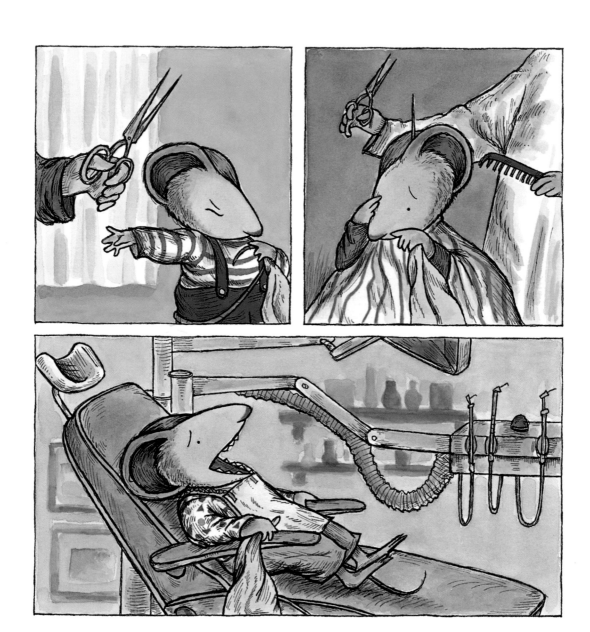

And Fuzzy was essential when it came to nail clippings

and haircuts and trips to the dentist.

"Can't be a baby forever," said Mrs. Tweezers.

"Haven't you heard of the vinegar trick?"

Owen's parents hadn't.

Mrs. Tweezers filled them in.

When Owen wasn't looking, his father dipped Owen's favorite corner of Fuzzy into a jar of vinegar.

Owen sniffed it and smelled it and sniffed it.

He picked a new favorite corner.

Then he rubbed the smelly corner all around his sandbox,
buried it in the garden, and dug it up again.

"Good as new," said Owen.

Fuzzy wasn't very fuzzy anymore.

But Owen didn't mind.

He carried it.

And wore it.

And dragged it.

He sucked it.

And hugged it.

And twisted it.

"What are we going to do?" asked Owen's mother.

"School is starting soon," said Owen's father.

"Can't bring a blanket to school," said Mrs. Tweezers.

"Haven't you heard of saying no?"

Owen's parents hadn't.

Mrs. Tweezers filled them in.

"I *have* to bring Fuzzy to school," said Owen.

"No," said Owen's mother.

"No," said Owen's father.

Owen buried his face in Fuzzy.

He started to cry and would not stop.

"Don't worry," said Owen's mother.

"It'll be all right," said Owen's father.

And then suddenly Owen's mother said, "I have an idea!"

It was an absolutely wonderful, positively perfect, especially terrific idea.

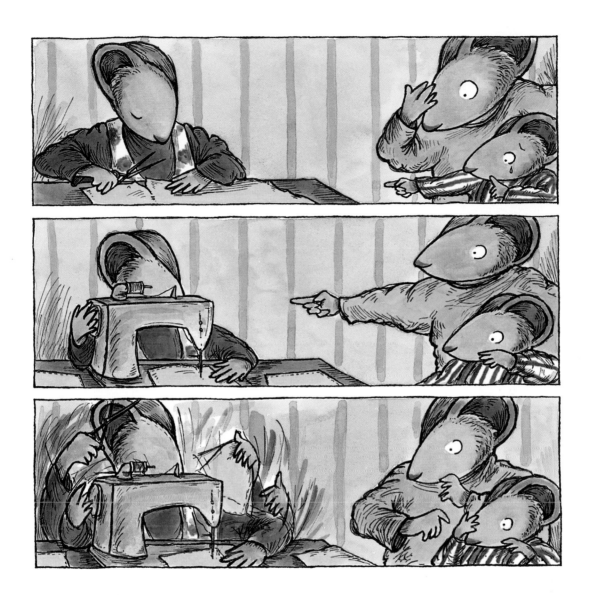

First she snipped.

And then she sewed.

Then she snipped again and sewed some more.

Snip, snip, snip.

Sew, sew, sew.

"Dry your eyes."

"Wipe your nose."

Hooray, hooray, hooray!

Now Owen carries one of his not-so-fuzzy handkerchiefs with him wherever he goes....

And Mrs. Tweezers doesn't say a thing.

LILLY'S PURPLE PLASTIC PURSE

BY KEVIN HENKES

GREENWILLOW BOOKS, NEW YORK

I LOVE SCHOOL!

LILLY loved school.

She loved the pointy pencils.

She loved the squeaky chalk.

And she loved the way her boots
went clickety-clickety-click
down the long, shiny hallways.

Lilly loved the privacy
of her very own desk.

She loved the fish sticks
and chocolate milk
every Friday
in the lunchroom.

And, most of all,
she loved her teacher,
Mr. Slinger.

Mr. Slinger was as sharp as a tack.
He wore artistic shirts.
He wore glasses on a chain around his neck.
And he wore a different colored tie
for each day of the week.

"Wow," said Lilly. That was just about all she could say. "Wow."

Instead of "Greetings, students"
or "Good morning, pupils,"
Mr. Slinger winked and said, "Howdy!"

He thought that desks in rows
were old-fashioned and boring.
"Do you rodents think you
can handle a semicircle?"

And he always provided
the most tasty snacks—
things that were curly
and crunchy and cheesy.

"I want to be a teacher
when I grow up," said Lilly.
"Me, too!" said her friends
Chester and Wilson and Victor.

At home Lilly pretended to be Mr. Slinger.

"I am the teacher," she told her baby brother, Julius. "Listen up!"

Lilly even wanted her own set of deluxe picture encyclopedias.

"What's with Lilly?" asked her mother.

"I thought she wanted to be a surgeon or an ambulance driver or a diva," said her father.

"It must be because of her new teacher, Mr. Slinger," said her mother.

"Wow," said her father. That was just about all he could say. "Wow."

Whenever the students had free time, they were permitted to go
to the Lightbulb Lab in the back of the classroom.

They expressed their ideas creatively through drawing and writing.

Lilly went often.

She had a *lot* of ideas.

She drew pictures of Mr. Slinger.

And she wrote stories about him, too.

During Sharing Time, Lilly showed her creations to the entire class.

"Wow," said Mr. Slinger. That was just about all he could say. "Wow."

When Mr. Slinger had bus duty, Lilly stood in line even though she didn't ride the bus.

CALL ON ME! PLEASE! PLEASE!

Lilly raised her hand
more than anyone else in class
(even if she didn't know the answer).

And she volunteered to stay
after school to clap erasers.

"I want to be a teacher
when I grow up," said Lilly.
"Excellent choice," said Mr. Slinger.

One Monday morning Lilly came to school especially happy.
She had gone shopping with her Grammy over the weekend.
Lilly had a new pair of movie star sunglasses, complete with
glittery diamonds and a chain like Mr. Slinger's.
She had three shiny quarters.
And, best of all, she had a brand new purple plastic purse
that played a jaunty tune when it was opened.

Lilly wanted to show everyone.
"Not now," said Mr. Slinger.
"Listen to our story."
Lilly had a hard time listening.

SHHH

Lilly *really* wanted to show everyone.
"Not now," said Mr. Slinger.
"Let's be considerate of our classmates."
Lilly had a hard time being considerate.

mice
nice
rice
dice

— LICE

Lilly *really, really* wanted to show everyone.
"Not now," said Mr. Slinger.
"Wait until recess or Sharing Time."
But Lilly could not wait.

TYPES OF CHEESE
SWISS
CHEDDAR
ROMANO
PROVOLONE

SHE'S IN TROUBLE.

The glasses were so glittery.
The quarters were so shiny.
And the purse played such
nice music, not to mention
how excellent it was for
storing school supplies.

"Look," Lilly whispered fiercely.
"Look, everyone. Look what I've got!"
Everyone looked.
Including Mr. Slinger.
He was not amused.

"I'll just keep your things at my desk until the end of the day," said Mr. Slinger. "They'll be safe there, and then you can take them home."

Lilly's stomach lurched.
She felt like crying.
Her glasses were gone.
Her quarters were gone.
Her purple plastic purse was gone.
Lilly longed for her purse all morning.
She was even too sad to eat the snack
Mr. Slinger served before recess.

That afternoon Lilly went to the Lightbulb Lab.

She was still very sad.

She thought and she thought and she thought.

And then she became angry.

She thought and she thought and she thought some more.

And then she became furious.

She thought and she thought and she thought a bit longer.

And then she drew a picture of Mr. Slinger.

Right before the last bell rang, Lilly sneaked the drawing
into Mr. Slinger's book bag.

When all the students were buttoned and zipped and snapped
and tied and ready to go home, Mr. Slinger strolled over to
Lilly and gave her purple plastic purse back.

"It's a beautiful purse," said Mr. Slinger. "Your quarters are nice
and jingly. And those glasses are absolutely fabulous. You may
bring them back to school as long as you don't disturb the rest
of the class."

"I do not want to be a teacher when I grow up," Lilly said
as she marched out of the classroom.

On the way home Lilly opened her purse.
Her glasses and quarters were inside.
And so was a note from Mr. Slinger. It said:
    "Today was a difficult day.
      Tomorrow will be better."
There was also a small bag of tasty snacks
at the bottom of the purse.

Lilly's stomach lurched.
She felt like crying.
She felt simply awful.

Lilly ran all the way home and told her mother and father everything.

Instead of watching her favorite cartoons, Lilly decided
to sit in the uncooperative chair.

I'LL STAY
HERE A
MILLION
YEARS FOR
MR. SLINGER.

WHY DOES
EVERYTHING
ALWAYS HAPPEN
TO ME?

ONE THOUSAND FIFTY-ONE,
ONE THOUSAND
FIFTY-TWO,
ONE THOUSAND
NINETY-NINE...

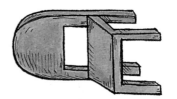

That night Lilly drew a new picture of Mr. Slinger
and wrote a story about him, too.

Lilly was really really Sorry.
So everyone forgave her.
Even her parents.
Even her stinky baby brother.
Even her especially incredible
            teacher.

And then the sun shined its
Smiley face down on
everyone and everything.
Even the bugs and worms.

THE END

Listen up!!!
I forgive
Everyone!!!

Kind Good
Nice
←could
be
principal

I am really really really really really really really really SORRY!!!

LILLY

worms
bugs→
←oops

I'M
AN
AUTHOR!

Lilly's mother wrote a note.

And Lilly's father baked some tasty snacks for Lilly to take
to school the next day.

"I think Mr. Slinger will understand," said Lilly's mother.

"I know he will," said Lilly's father.

The next morning Lilly got to school early.

"These are for you," Lilly said to Mr. Slinger.

"Because I'm really, really, really, really, really, really, really, really, really, really, really, really, really, really, really, really, really, really sorry."

Mr. Slinger read the story.

And he looked at the picture.

And he read the note.

And he sampled the snacks.

"Wow," said Mr. Slinger. That was just about all he could say. "Wow."

"What do you think we should do with this?" asked Mr. Slinger.

"Could we just throw it away?" asked Lilly.

"Excellent idea," said Mr. Slinger.

During Sharing Time, Lilly demonstrated the many uses and unique qualities of her purple plastic purse, her shiny quarters, and her glittery movie star sunglasses.

Then she did a little performance using them as props.

"It's called Interpretive Dance," said Lilly.

Mr. Slinger joined in.

"Wow," said the entire class. That was just about all they could say. "Wow."

Throughout the rest of the day, Lilly's purse and quarters
and sunglasses were tucked safely inside her desk.
She peeked at them often but did not disturb a soul.

Right before the last bell rang, Mr. Slinger served Lilly's snacks,
to everyone's delight.

"What do you want to be when you grow up?" asked Mr. Slinger.

"A TEACHER!" everyone responded. Lilly's response was
the loudest.

"Excellent choice," said Mr. Slinger.

As the pupils filed out of the classroom,
Lilly held her purple plastic purse close to her heart.
Mr. Slinger was right—it *had* been a better day.

Lilly ran and skipped and hopped and flew all the way home, she was so happy.

And she really *did* want to be a teacher when she grew up—

That is, when she didn't want to be a dancer
or a surgeon or an ambulance driver or a diva
or a pilot or a hairdresser or a scuba diver . . .

Wemberly Worried

KEVIN HENKES

GREENWILLOW BOOKS
An Imprint of HarperCollinsPublishers

Wemberly worried about everything.

Big things,

I WANTED
TO MAKE SURE
YOU WERE
STILL HERE.

little things,

and things in between.

Wemberly worried in the morning.

She worried at night.

And she worried throughout the day.

"You worry too much," said her mother.

"When you worry, I worry," said her father.

"Worry, worry, worry," said her grandmother.

"Too much worry."

At home, Wemberly worried

about the tree in the front yard,

WHAT IF IT FALLS ON OUR HOUSE?

and the crack

in the living room wall,

and the noise the radiators made.

At the playground, Wemberly worried about

the chains on the swings,

and the bolts on the slide,

and the bars on the jungle gym.

And always, she worried about her doll, Petal.

"Don't worry," said her mother.

"Don't worry," said her father.

But Wemberly worried.

She worried and worried and worried.

When Wemberly was especially worried, she rubbed Petal's ears.

Wemberly worried that if she didn't stop worrying,

Petal would have no ears left at all.

On her birthday, Wemberly worried

that no one would come to her party.

"See," said her mother, "there was nothing to worry about."

THIS IS THE
BEST PRESENT
EVER!

I WISH I HAD MY
BIRTHDAY TODAY.

But then Wemberly worried that there wouldn't be enough cake.

On Halloween, Wemberly worried
that there would be too many
butterflies in the neighborhood parade.

"See," said her father, "there was nothing to worry about."

But then Wemberly worried because she was the only one.

"You worry too much," said her mother.

"When you worry, I worry," said her father.

"Worry, worry, worry," said her grandmother.

"Too much worry."

Soon, Wemberly had a new worry: school.

Wemberly worried about the start of school

more than anything she had ever worried about before.

By the time the first day arrived, Wemberly had a long list of worries.

What if no one else has spots?

What if no one else wears stripes?

What if no one else brings a doll?

What if the teacher is mean?

What if the room smells bad?

★ 244 ★

What if they
make fun
of my name?

What if I can't
find the bathroom?

What if I hate
the snack?

What if
I have
to cry?

"Don't worry," said her mother.

"Don't worry," said her father.

But Wemberly worried.

She worried and worried and worried.

She worried all the way there.

HAVE FUN!

While Wemberly's parents talked to the teacher, Mrs. Peachum,
Wemberly looked around the room.

Then Mrs. Peachum said, "Wemberly, there is someone
I think you should meet."

Her name was Jewel.

She was standing by herself.

She was wearing stripes.

She was holding a doll.

At first, Wemberly and Jewel just peeked at each other.

"This is Petal," said Wemberly.

"This is Nibblet," said Jewel.

Petal waved.

Nibblet waved back.

"Hi," said Petal.

"Hi," said Nibblet.

"I rub her ears," said Wemberly.

"I rub her nose," said Jewel.

Throughout the morning, Wemberly and Jewel

sat side by side and played together whenever they could.

Petal and Nibblet sat side by side, too.

Wemberly worried.

But no more than usual.

And sometimes even less.

Before Wemberly knew it,

it was time to go home.

"Come back tomorrow," called Mrs. Peachum,

as the students walked out the door.

Wemberly turned and smiled and waved.

"I will," she said. "Don't worry."

Lilly's Big Day

KEVIN HENKES

Greenwillow Books

An Imprint of HarperCollins Publishers

One day Lilly's teacher, Mr. Slinger, announced to the class
that he was going to marry Ms. Shotwell, the school nurse.
Lilly's heart leaped. She had always wanted to be a flower girl.
"It will be the biggest day of my life," said Mr. Slinger.
"Mine, too," whispered Lilly.

At home in her room, Lilly practiced being a flower girl.

First she changed into something more appropriate.

Then she held her head high

and smiled brightly

and raised her eyebrows

and turned her head from side to side

and carried her hands proudly in front of her

and hummed "Here Comes the Bride"

and walked the length of her room very, very slowly.

Back and forth, back and forth, back and forth.

"It will be the biggest day of my life," said Lilly.

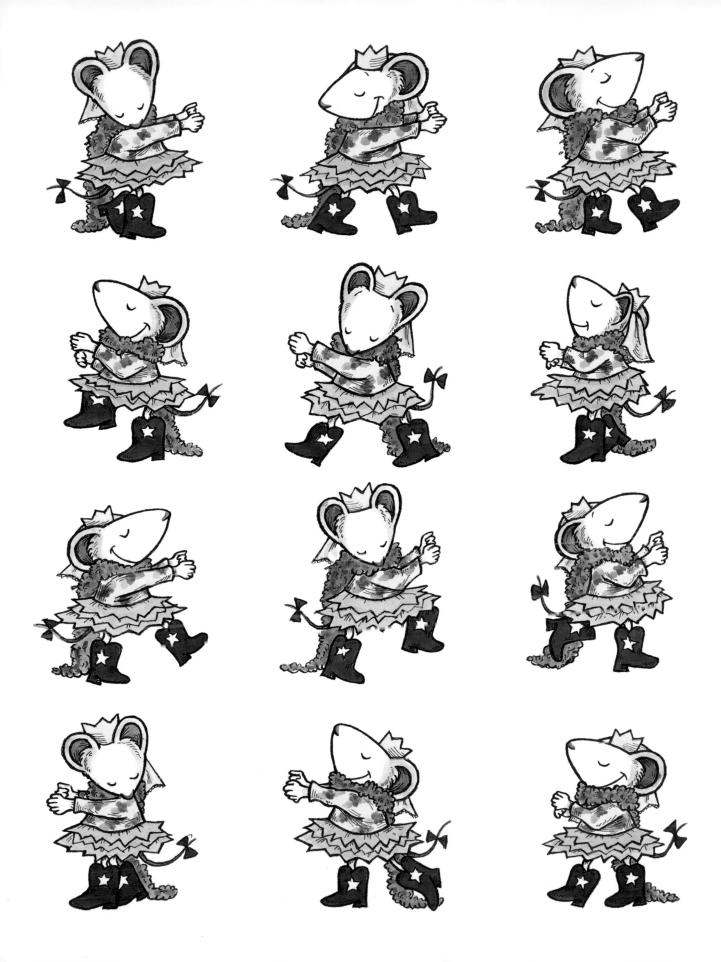

"Who are you pretending to be tonight?"
asked Lilly's mother at dinner.

"I'm not pretending," said Lilly. "I'm a flower girl."

"Who's getting married?" asked her father.

"Mr. Slinger," said Lilly.

"Really?" said her mother.

"Really?" said her father.

"Really," said Lilly. "He's going to marry Ms. Shotwell.
   He told us today. And I'm going to be the flower girl."
"You are?" said her father.
"Did Mr. Slinger ask you?" said her mother.
"Not yet," said Lilly.

At bedtime Lilly's mother said, "Lilly, there are so many students in your class. Mr. Slinger couldn't possibly pick just one to be a flower girl."

Her father said, "It wouldn't be fair."

"He probably has a niece . . . ," said her mother.

"Maybe Aunt Mona will get married someday . . . ," said her father.

"Do you understand what we're trying to say?" asked her mother.

Lilly nodded.

"Are you sure?" asked her father.

Lilly nodded again.

After her parents left her room, Lilly said, "I understand that I'm going to be a flower girl."

The next day at school during Sharing Time, Lilly said, "I've always wanted to be a flower girl. Even more than a surgeon or a diva or a hairdresser."

The following afternoon when Mr. Slinger had recess duty, Lilly picked a handful of weeds at the edge of the playground. She carried the weeds proudly in front of her and walked very, very slowly past Mr. Slinger until the bell rang. Back and forth, back and forth, back and forth.

And the morning after that, Lilly went to the Lightbulb Lab in the back of the classroom. She drew a self-portrait.

Mr. Slinger called Lilly up to his desk during Quiet Reading Time. "Lilly," he said, "I can tell that you want to be a flower girl, but unfortunately my niece, Ginger, is going to be the flower girl at my wedding."
Lilly's heart sank.

"But," said Mr. Slinger, "I also want you to know that everyone in the class will be invited to the wedding. We can all dance together at the reception. It'll be fun."
Lilly's stomach hurt.
"This seems really important to you," said Mr. Slinger.
Lilly's cheeks turned pink.

"You know . . . ," said Mr. Slinger, "I was just thinking that you might like to be Ginger's assistant. You could stand with her and keep her company until she has to walk down the aisle. You could make sure her dress isn't crooked and that she holds her flowers properly."

Lilly considered this.

"You could remind her to walk slowly," said Mr. Slinger.

Lilly considered some more.

"You could wear a corsage," said Mr. Slinger.

"Oh, all right," said Lilly, "if you really need me so much."

Lilly tried to get excited about being Ginger's assistant.

"Weddings wouldn't even exist without flower girl assistants,"
she told her baby brother, Julius.

"I have a special responsibility," she told her parents.

When her Grammy took her shopping for a new dress for the wedding, Lilly told the clerk, "A flower girl assistant is *very* important. Important *and* glamorous."

But when it really sank in that she would not be walking
down the aisle carrying a bouquet with everyone watching,
Lilly pretended that her teddy bear was Mr. Slinger.
She made him sit in the Uncooperative Chair.
"You can just stay there forever," she said.

As the wedding drew near, Mr. Slinger counted down the days on the chalkboard.

"One day closer to the biggest day of my life," he would say.

"One day closer to the biggest day of *Ginger's* life," Lilly would whisper.

And still, at home in her room, Lilly practiced.
 She held her head high
  and smiled brightly
   and raised her eyebrows
    and turned her head from side to side
     and carried her hands proudly in front of her
      and hummed "Here Comes the Bride"
       and walked the length of her room very, very slowly.
        Back and forth, back and forth, back and forth.

The day of the wedding finally arrived.
Lilly hoped and hoped that Ginger would have pinkeye
or a bad fever and not show up.
But she was there. And she was all ready. Her dress was
straight and she held her flowers properly.

"Are you sure you want to do this?" said Lilly.

"Yes," said Ginger.

"Are you sure you're sure?"

"Yes."

"Are you *really* sure you're sure?"

Lilly hoped and hoped that Ginger would change her mind.

But she didn't.

It was time for the ceremony to begin.

The music swelled.

Everyone stood.

The moment came for Ginger to walk down the aisle.

Ginger didn't move.

Mr. Slinger motioned her forward.

"Go," said Lilly.

Ginger was frozen.

"Now," said Lilly.

Ginger was as still as a stone.

"You can do it," said Lilly.

But Ginger couldn't.

Everyone waited. And waited. And waited.

No one knew what to do—except Lilly.

Lilly scooped up Ginger and said, "Here we go."

Then Lilly walked very, very slowly down the aisle.

She held her head high

and smiled brightly

and raised her eyebrows

and turned her head from side to side

and carried Ginger proudly in front of her.

When she reached Mr. Slinger, everyone clapped.
"I knew this would be the biggest day of my life!" said Lilly.

★ 284 ★

Lilly was so excited she barely noticed the rest of the ceremony.

The reception was great fun.

After the cake was served, Lilly coached Ginger for the next time she would be a flower girl.

"I won't be with you at every wedding," said Lilly. "I won't be able to save you every time."

Together they walked back and forth,
back and forth,
back and forth,
very, very slowly.

Soon they were dancing.

And soon after that, they were joined by Chester, Wilson,
Victor, Julius, Mr. Slinger, Ms. Shotwell, and many others.
"It's Interpretive Dance!" said Mr. Slinger.
"We're doing the Flower Girl!" said Lilly.

Lilly's family stayed at the reception until Lilly was perfectly exhausted.

"But there's something I have to do before we go," said Lilly.

She needed to find Ginger one last time.

And when she did, she said, "Ginger, when I get married,
you can be my flower girl."

Sharing Lilly & Friends with Your Young Child

These cherished stories have been delighting children and their parents, grandparents, teachers, and caregivers for more than thirty years. Kevin Henkes, beloved author and illustrator, has a natural gift for exploring the emotional lives of young children. His books consider the major traumas and transitions in a young child's life—accepting a new sibling, starting school, coping with a bully—and offer resolutions not only wise and understandable but entertaining as well. He writes (seemingly without effort, but that's part of the magic of it) of universal truths and individual triumphs.

Perhaps it is the characters who make these stories so endearing and unforgettable. They are mice, yes, but they are fully relatable, unique, and sympathetic; they are also fearless and fearful, worried and precise; and one in particular marches across the page with a confident exuberance that sometimes gets her in trouble. In these deceivingly simple stories, Kevin Henkes reveals character subtly by "showing," never "telling." In *Chester's Way*, the reader comes to understand Chester and Wilson by the many ways they interact with each other even before they meet Lilly, causing Chester's mother to say, "They really are two peas in a pod."

The stories never talk down to children; their personalities and emotions are recognized as valid. As Mr. Slinger writes to Lilly, "Today was a difficult day. Tomorrow will be better." And Owen's mother comes up with an "absolutely wonderful, positively perfect, especially terrific idea" that honors Owen's feelings while solving the problem.

Like Mr. Slinger and Owen's mother, the adults in Kevin Henkes's books are wise and supportive; and the mouse parents share equally in the raising of their children. They offer reassuring advice but are often perplexed at a child's behavior, just like human caregivers. Chrysanthemum's father resorts to reading books about Childhood Anxiety to cope with his daughter's changing feelings about her name. The parents in a Kevin Henkes book may be sympathetic and even indulgent to childhood predicaments, but bad behavior has its consequences. Lilly is a frequent visitor to the "uncooperative chair." But there is often self-realization on the part of a Henkes character as well, an important skill for young children to learn and internalize. After realizing she has offended Mr. Slinger, Lilly voluntarily puts herself in the uncooperative chair.

In some cases, the adults in *Lilly & Friends* are instrumental in a story's resolution. Owen's mother devises a way to recycle the fuzzy blanket; and that "indescribable wonder," the very pregnant and enthusiastic music teacher, Mrs. Delphinium Twinkle, gives Chrysanthemum a reason to be proud of her name again. But often it is the child who finds a solution. When Sophie has had enough of Wendell, with a determined look in her eye she turns the garden hose on her naughty guest. What starts out as revenge becomes a playful game—lesson learned, but in the gentlest of ways.

Yes, these are the gentlest of stories, yet they are imbued with such genuine wisdom and humor as to make them pleasurable reading experiences to be enjoyed again and again.

Here are some ways to share *Lilly & Friends* with the children in your life:

Reading Aloud

In the 1985 landmark report *Becoming a Nation of Readers*, the top recommendation stated: "Parents should read to preschool children and informally teach them about reading and writing. Reading to children, discussing stories and experiences with them, are practices that are consistently associated with eventual success in reading."[1] In the years since, the research has been clear in reinforcing the recommendation that the simple act of reading aloud to a child is the best known way to build vocabulary, develop comprehension, and help make your child a reader. But reading aloud is not just about developing literacy skills. This unique shared experience can also build a special bond between the child and the

reader. Picture books will help you get to know the child in your care better and give you insight into what they are thinking by how they respond to a particular story. Plus, reading together is always a good excuse for a cozy quiet time.

SOME TIPS:

* Start reading to your baby early, and read often
* Try to find a time with the fewest distractions. Bedtime is a natural, but look for other opportunities during the day—even the waiting room at the doctor's office!
* Encourage the child to select the book, hold it, and turn the pages
* Read with expression—have fun taking on the persona of nosy Mrs. Tweezers from *Owen*, or the fearful little sister Louise from *Sheila Rae, the Brave*
* Follow the words with your finger, so the child can see the words as well as hear them
* Look at the pictures as you read, and talk about them
* Give the child time to ask questions and make comments

Talk about or Explain Unfamiliar Words

New words can stretch a child's vocabulary, and the rich language in the stories in *Lilly & Friends* offers many opportunities for exploration. *Chrysanthemum* is a challenging word to pronounce, and the book is full of complex language. The family plays Parcheesi (a little pun) and at one point the father, in response to the teasing Chrysanthemum is experiencing, says, "And envious and begrudging and discontented and jaundiced." Here is an opportunity to investigate and explain these exciting-sounding new words. Have a pad or easel handy to write them out slowly and refer to them in repeated readings.

Look for Patterns

Repetitious language or story patterns help children respond and engage easily as they join in on refrains or predict action. In Kevin Henkes's mouse stories there are many examples of repetitive patterns to support emergent readers, those children just getting ready to read. In *Wemberly Worried,* for example, a reassuring chorus of family members proclaims:

"You worry too much," said her mother.

"When you worry, I worry," said her father.

"Worry, worry, worry," said her grandmother. "Too much worry."

Chances are, the second time you read *Wemberly Worried*, your child will chime in with the word "worry" at just the right moment.

Let Your Child Tell the Story

Children love to hear a favorite story again and again. When a story becomes familiar, pre-readers often like to "read" the story themselves. Recalling the story helps the child better understand a text or remember events. The art and page layout in these stories make it easy for the child to tell the story in their own words. For example, *Chrysanthemum* uses many small panels to move the action forward, and the art often mirrors what is happening in the text. Look at the page of nine small squares depicting Chrysanthemum from the time she was a baby. This is a welcoming place for the child viewer to describe what is happening in each mini-illustration.

Make Reading Aloud a Shared Experience

Although reading the story straight through while a child listens has its benefits, such as developing listening skills, children get more out of a book when they are actively involved. Shared reading is often called dialogic reading, which means having a dialogue with a child around the text you are reading. Shared or dialogic reading can be as simple as stopping when a child has a question or observation about the story; for example, if your child says, "I don't like Wendell," it offers the opportunity for the adult to ask, "What is it about Wendell that makes you say that?" The stories in *Lilly & Friends* abound with opportunities for shared reading. The plots and the ways in which the characters develop allow room for interpretation—not all behaviors and motivations are obvious. You yourself may not know the answer to a question, making the discussion even more open-ended. One example (from *Sheila Rae, the Brave*) might be: "How was Sheila Rae's little sister, Louise, able to find her way home?" This type of questioning develops an important literacy skill—comprehension, or understanding the meaning of the story.

If you notice that your child looks puzzled by something in the story, you can also ask a question to clarify a point or to expand interpretation. Often these are open-ended "what" or "why" questions.

SOME EXAMPLES MIGHT BE:

* What do you think Mrs. Tweezers means by telling Owen's parents about the blanket fairy?
* Why do you think Wilson and Chester like to do the same things together?
* What do you think Lilly's parents mean when they say, "Julius is the baby of the world"?

Read the Pictures

There are many ways to enjoy a book and one is to take a "picture book walk," where the child focuses on the pictures to provide or predict meaning. Kevin Henkes's illustrations in *Lilly & Friends* are detailed and playful, and a thoughtful layout and design makes these stories especially appropriate for "picture book walks." For example, when Owen's mother snips Fuzzy into handkerchiefs, in *Owen*, we see nine small panels of Owen doing . . . what? Ask your child, "What do you see? What is this picture telling you?" The clear body language and expressions in these pictures allow the viewer to interpret meaning. When Lilly discovers the note from Mr. Slinger in her purse in *Lilly's Purple Plastic Purse*, the child might ask, "Why are the pictures of Lilly getting smaller?" As a response try asking, "Why do you think this is happening?" Looking at settings, body language, and facial expressions allows the child to make predictions about what might happen. When Ginger, in *Lilly's Big Day*, freezes before walking down the aisle, ask your child, "What do you think will happen?"

Explore Emotional Themes in the Books

Caregivers often turn to books when a child has a particular need, such as a negative reaction to a new sibling or first-day-of-school jitters. And books such as *Julius, the Baby of the World* and *Wemberly Worried* can offer a positive way for adults to talk with children in their care about concerns and fears. But reading these stories *before* there is a new baby in the house or *before* one has to face that first day of school is equally important. Books can offer children the vicarious experience of getting lost, like Sheila Rae in *Sheila Rae, the Brave*, or being too terrified to walk down the aisle as a flower girl, like Ginger in *Lilly's Big Day*, before actually facing such events or events like them. Reading about others who have had experiences and witnessing the way in which they solve their problems will better prepare a child for life's challenges when they do happen. Kevin Henkes's books also explore a range of social, emotional, and developmental qualities that are important for children to experience. Children will learn from Lilly as she struggles to manage her temper and develop a self-awareness about her actions, while still remaining her ebullient self. They will see how Chrysanthemum develops confidence and self-esteem in the face of bullying behavior. Think of these stories as being bite-sized dress rehearsals for life.

Connect the Stories to Your Child's Life

You can extend the meaning and impact of these stories even further by asking children questions that help them connect their own experiences to incidents in the books. This helps children form a bridge between the text and their real world. Reading any one of the stories in *Lilly & Friends* might trigger a real-life connection. Wemberly worries about the first day of school—"Do you remember how you felt on the first day of school?" is a question to ask. Perhaps *A Weekend with Wendell* will start a conversation about a friend or relative who came to visit and wasn't the best-behaved guest. You can also ask questions that prompt the child in your care to reflect on the stories. "How would you have solved the problem of Owen refusing to give up his fuzzy blanket?"

Art & Writing Activities

"The Lightbulb Lab—Where Great Ideas Are Born" is a place in the back of Lilly's classroom where "students can express their ideas creatively through drawing and writing." Lilly often visits the Lightbulb Lab to write stories and draw pictures about her feelings. Set up your own Lightbulb Lab with some simple supplies, and encourage your child to design a poster about one of the characters in *Lilly & Friends*. If there is a new baby in the house, for example, draw a picture for the baby's room.

The mouse homes in *Lilly & Friends* are filled with art, some inspired by real artists. The characters also like to draw—there are drawings on Sophie's walls, and Wendell uses her crayons to draw a mean "See You Tomorrow" picture. Almost any character or situation in any of these stories can be the inspiration for a drawing; for example, draw a map of the new way home taken by Sheila Rae and her sister. Or, draw a picture of Mrs. Delphinium Twinkle's garden.

Imaginative and Real Play

The characters in *Lilly & Friends*, especially Lilly, love to dress up in disguises and engage in imaginative play. Keep a costume box nearby for dress-up; this is an entertaining way for your child to extend a story by participating in similar activities. And it doesn't need to be fancy!

In *Lilly's Purple Plastic Purse*, Lilly performs an interpretive dance with her noisy props, and again, after the wedding in *Lilly's Big Day*, she creates an interpretive dance she calls the Flower Girl Dance. Discuss the meaning of interpretive dance, then put on some fun music and do the flower girl dance (you can follow the steps Lilly creates in the book), or another dance of your choice or creation.

Wemberly in *Wemberly Worried* is dressed as a butterfly for Halloween—look again at the other costumes in the neighborhood parade. Did you spot Lilly? What are others dressed up as? What is your favorite Halloween costume? Try making a costume of your own!

A classic is often described as a treasured book that a child can delight in returning to over and over again. Surely then, the beloved stories in *Lilly & Friends* have attained this status. Funny and affecting, these stories reveal different layers of appreciation and meaning with each rereading. While firmly grounded in the world of childhood, friends, and family, the stories in *Lilly & Friends* offer an enduring wisdom that resonates with both children and adults and transcends the here-and-now. Enjoy sharing these classics with the child in your life.

—*Caroline Ward*

1. Richard C. Anderson, et al., *Becoming a Nation of Readers: The Report of the Commission on Reading* (Illinois University, Urbana, Center for the Study of Reading. National Academy of Education, Washington, D.C., 1985). https://files.eric.ed.gov/fulltext/ED253865.pdf

Afterword

When Virginia Duncan, my editor; Paul Zakris, my art director; and I placed my mouse picture books on a table to discuss this treasury, I had a strong reaction. It was an emotional experience for me. I rarely, if ever, look at the books as a group, and when we did, I felt as if my life had been laid out before me.

I was twenty-four years old when I wrote and illustrated *A Weekend with Wendell*, the first of the nine books included here, and forty-five years old when *Lilly's Big Day*, the last, was published in 2006. I'd gone from being newly married to being a parent. I'd created the books in four different homes.

Working on these books brought me joy and provided anchors in my life during the times in which I was working on them. And they remind me of people I know and love and of events from my life that stand out.

I have a niece who had a blanket she loved deeply, when she was little. She was the inspiration for *Owen*. And her relationship with her older sister informed *Julius, the Baby of the World*.

I begged for a pair of cowboy boots when I was a boy. My parents let me get them, but I quickly discovered that they were too flashy for me, and I never wore them out of the house. I gave them to Lilly because I knew she could handle them.

When I was growing up, I had a neighbor named Sheila Rae and a neighbor very much like my character Mrs. Tweezers. They've long been out of my life, but they live on in my books.

My now-grown daughter's wish to be a flower girl was never fulfilled, but I got a book out of her longing (*Lilly's Big Day*), and I dedicated it to her.

I am a worrier and when I wrote the first draft of *Wemberly Worried*, my wife and I were staying at her mother's house on Wemberly Way in Springfield, Oregon. It struck me with absolute certainty that my heroine's perfect name was right before me, on the street sign in the front yard, waiting to be claimed.

All these bits and pieces of life need to be combined with imagination and given form if they are to be successful books. So, this treasury represents years of work and years of living in my head. Years that have been wildly fulfilling for me. I cannot imagine any other type of work that would have been better suited to me and how I wanted to live my life.

I think of my books as being about ordinary things. Ordinary things are what interest me most, what I'm drawn to when I'm writing. So, it makes sense that my books are about common experiences: what it feels like to be bullied, what it feels like to need a security object, what it feels like to find a new friend, what it feels like to get a new sibling, what it feels like to start school, what it feels like to love a teacher.

I'm often asked which book is my favorite. It's difficult to say. Each is my favorite in its own way. Each reflects the very best I was capable of at the time I wrote and illustrated it. Wendell, Chester, Lilly, Owen, Chrysanthemum, Wemberly—I love them all.

The question I'm asked most often is: Why mice? Of course, the mice are children. But I enjoy drawing animals more than I do humans. And, I've found that I can heighten the humor and dramatize the situations in the texts using my mice in a way that wouldn't be funny if carried out with their human counterparts. For example, Lilly can pinch Julius's tail and yell in his ear and it works; similar actions carried out by realistically rendered humans wouldn't.

One of the wonders of my job is that my characters don't age. They are frozen in time. I've changed quite a bit since I wrote *A Weekend with Wendell*, but Wendell and Sophie have not. That's the way it is with books. Share a book with a child for the first time, and no matter how long ago the book was published, it is new.

One of my greatest joys over the years has been seeing how people have connected to my books and characters. I've met families with children named Lilly and Owen because of my books. I've seen tattoos of Lilly and Chrysanthemum—and even of Wemberly's doll, Petal. I've been told by many people that Mr. Slinger's words, "Today was a difficult day. Tomorrow will be better," have become part of their family's vernacular. Once, in public, I even overheard a mother ask her child, "Why are you being so Wemberlyish today?" This took place on a tiny island off the coast of Maine.

I imagine that the books in this treasury will be familiar to some, but that they will be new to others. And I hope that—new or familiar—children will like one or more of the stories enough to say: Read it again.

Read it again—the nicest thing for an author to hear.

Kevin Henkes

Kevin Henkes was born in Racine, Wisconsin, in 1960. When he was nineteen years old, he went to New York City to look for a publisher. Susan Hirschman, founder of Greenwillow Books, offered him a contract at their initial meeting. His first book, *All Alone*, was published in 1981. *A Weekend with Wendell*, the first book with his signature mouse characters, was published in 1986.

Kevin Henkes has written and illustrated more than fifty books, including board books, picture books, books for beginning readers, and novels, all published by Greenwillow Books.

Praised for both his writing and his illustrating, Kevin Henkes has been awarded the Caldecott Medal, two Caldecott Honors, two Newbery Honors, and two Geisel Honors. In 2020, Kevin Henkes was awarded the Children's Literature Legacy Award for lifetime achievement from the American Library Association. His books have been #1 *New York Times* bestsellers and have been translated into many languages. He lives in Madison, Wisconsin.

"Behind each book is a wide-open heart, one readers can't
help but respond to, that makes all of Henkes's books . . .
of special value to children."—*Publishers Weekly*

A Note from the Publisher

The art was prepared as full-color watercolor paintings combined with a black pen-and-ink line.

The first eight books were designed by Kevin Henkes and Ava Weiss.
Lilly's Big Day was designed by Kevin Henkes and Paul Zakris.

A special thanks to Caroline Ward, for her inspiring appreciation of
Kevin Henkes and her thoughts about sharing the stories in this treasury.

For more information about Kevin Henkes and his books, please visit www.kevinhenkes.com.

Caroline Ward has more than forty years of experience as a public library youth services librarian and adjunct professor of children's literature. She has chaired the Newbery Committee (1990) and the Geisel Award Committee (2006), and just completed a term on the 2019 Caldecott Committee. She is currently on the Bank Street Children's Book Committee and works as a youth literature consultant on special projects related to books and libraries.